W9-CGM-514

Filipino Children's Favorite Stories

Filipino Children's Favorite Stories

retold by liana romulo
illustrated by joanne de leon

PERIPLUS

Published by Periplus Editions (HK) Ltd
Text copyright © 2000 Liana Romulo
Illustrations copyright © 2000 Periplus Editions (HK) Ltd

All Rights Reserved. No part of this publication may be reproduced, stored in a retrieval system, or transmitted, in any form or by any means, electronic, mechanical, photocopying, recording or otherwise, without the prior written permission of the publisher.

ISBN 962-593-765-X (Hard Cover)
ISBN 962-593-887-7 (Paper Back) Printed in Singapore

Note from the author: Many thanks to Roda Novenario for helping me dig up several valuable sources of Philippine stories. I am also grateful to Ompong Remigio for her significant contributions to *Why Mosquitoes Buzz Around Our Ears*.

Editor Kim Inglis; design Loretta Reilly

Distributed by:
North America Tuttle Publishing, Distribution Center, Airport Industrial Park, 364 Innovation Drive, North Clarendon, VT 05759. tel (802) 773 8930 tel (800) 526 2778

Southeast Asia Berkeley Books Pte Ltd, 5 Little Road #08-01, Singapore 536983. tel (65) 280 3320 fax (65) 280 6290

Japan Tuttle Publishing, RK Building, 2nd Floor, 2-13-10 Shimo-Meguro, Meguro-Ku, Tokyo 153. tel (813) 5437 6171 fax (813) 5437 0755

Indonesia
PT Wira Mandala Pustaka, Jl Kelapa Gading Kirana, Blok A14 No 17, Jakarta 14240. tel (62) 21 451 5351 fax (62) 21 453 4987

Contents

Why Mosquitoes Buzz Around Our Ears

A long time ago, in a fishpond not far from the rice fields, there lived a giant crab named Maga. Maga was no ordinary crab. He was King of Crabs, and everyone was afraid of him. Not only was he always in a crabby mood, he was almost twice as big as his crab cousins. When Maga was mad, his big claws would go *Snap! Snap!* and everyone—the fish, fireflies, worms, frogs, mosquitoes, snails, birds—would run away.

One night, Maga couldn't fall asleep, which wasn't at all unusual. As everybody in the pond kingdom knew, Maga always had trouble sleeping. They also knew that if anyone dared wake him from his sleep, Maga would get very angry. That night he crept in and out of his house restlessly, trying to make himself tired enough to sleep. His house was a hole in the mud that led into a deep, dark tunnel underground. Finally, he gave up and decided to call for his old sheriff, who lived in a crab hole nearby. "Cagang!" he yelled into the quiet darkness. "Cagang!"

A while later Cagang arrived at Maga's side. Though Cagang was the sheriff, he was an old and brittle crab, and he could barely outrun a worm. "Yes, sir," he said, his grey feelers twitching. "What can I do for you, sir?"

"Gather up all the frogs you can find and bring them here," Maga said crankily. "I can't sleep, and I want them to sing to me." Several minutes later, Maga was back in his house, listening to the frogs sing.

> "*Kokak, kokak,*
> sit back, sit back.
> *Blideet, blideet,*
> now go to sleep,"
>
> > the frogs chorused.

Maga soon fell into a deep, deep sleep.

> *Snooorrrrkkkk* . . .
> *Snooorrrrkkkk* . . .
> *Whrrssh* . . .
> *Whrrssh* . . .
>
> > he snored loudly.

Cagang began to feel a bit sleepy, himself, so he, too, crawled into his own hole to go to sleep for the night.

> "*Kokak, kokak,*
> sit back, sit back.
> *Blideet, blideet,*
> now go to sleep,"
>
> > the frogs went on singing.

Cagang returned at noon, the firefly nervously fluttering beside him. "Whatever it is," she said tremulously, "I swear I didn't do it."

"Be quiet!" Maga said, fuming. The heat from the sun was now beating down on his back, and he was growing madder and madder by the minute.

"Firefly, explain why—"

Snap! Snap! Snap!

"—you were carrying fire near the snail's house last night."

The firefly's wings suddenly went still, and her face dimmed. She was so scared, she couldn't move.

"I-I-I—" she began,

"Well, speak, firefly!" Maga said impatiently. "I haven't got all day."

"I-I-I—" the firefly tried again. "I had to turn on my fire to keep the mosquito away," she explained. "He was trying to bite me."

The firefly's story seemed perfectly believable to Maga, but before he could give Cagang the order to arrest the mosquito, the old sheriff spoke up. "You want me to find the mosquito and arrest him, sir?" he said, sounding tired.

"Bring him to me now!" he raged, rapidly snapping his pincers.

Snap! Snap! Snap! Snap!

Cagang dutifully took off in search of the mosquito, as the firefly fluttered away. Late in the afternoon, he returned with the humming mosquito.

"Well, hello, King," the mosquito said. "Why have you invited me here?" Then he casually buzzed over to where Maga was sitting.

Maga didn't like the mosquito's tone one bit. He didn't even seem afraid.

Snap! Snap! Snap!

went his claws threateningly.

Snap! Snap!

"Why were you trying to bite the firefly?"

The mosquito laughed, buzzing even closer to Maga. "I'm a mosquito, aren't I?" he said cockily. "It's what I do."

"You will be punished!" Maga roared, his eyes bulging.

Then the mosquito flew swiftly up into the air and poked Maga right in the eye. He knew that the eyes were the only soft parts of the crab.

"Aaaah!" Maga cried, turning bright red.

"Cagang!" he screamed. "Kill that little bug!"

By this time, Cagang was truly exhausted. But he mustered up all his strength and raised his pincers. *Snip!* went one of his claws weakly. *Snip, snip.*

The mosquito laughed and laughed, even daring to fly in between Cagang's claws just for the fun of it. In and out he recklessly flew until, suddenly, Cagang caught him with one deadly snip. The mosquito stopped laughing and fell to the ground, lifeless.

Then, out of nowhere came a battalion of mosquitoes with a humming roar. *Bzzz, Bzzzz, Buzzz!* Hundreds of the dead mosquito's friends surrounded Maga and the poor old sheriff, poking them in the eyes with their sharp stingers.

Snip! Snap! Snap! the crabs fought back. But Maga's powerful claws were useless to him. The mosquitoes were just too fast and too small.

Finally, Maga and Cagang gave up and scampered into their holes, with the mosquito battalion trailing close behind.

The mosquitoes could no longer get to Maga and Cagang, who were safely burrowed in their houses deep underground. But, today, a thousand years later, the mosquitoes are still waiting for them to come out. So, whenever they see the holes of our ears, they're reminded of Maga's and Cagang's crab holes.

And that's why mosquitoes buzz around our ears.

The Terrible Giant

"Please don't hurt me!" Tutubi the Dragonfly said, trembling.

But Lupit, the mean, ugly giant only laughed. "Ha, ha, ha, ha!"

He was as tall as the tallest coconut tree, and he was holding Tutubi up close to his hairy face, her delicate tail caught between his thumb and forefinger.

She looked into one of his big black eyes. "I beg you," she said, shaking with fear. "Please leave me alone."

Lupit laughed once again, the deep sound of his voice thundering over the rolling green hills. "You have such pretty wings," he said. "You don't need two of them, do you?" With that, he plucked off one of her transparent wings.

"Aaaah!" she screamed.

Then suddenly she felt herself tumbling through the air and into the grass. The giant had tossed her aside, and now he was heading for his house at the top of the hill. He had a big house, but he lived all by himself because all the creatures in the countryside hated him. Lupit liked to cut off lizards' tails, stomp on anthills, and trap butterflies in plastic bags, for no reason at all.

Soon Ahas the Snake slithered by and found Tutubi trapped among the tall weeds. Crying, she told him what Lupit had done. Ahas grew very angry. "He must be punished," he said. "I have had enough of his cruelty!"

Tutubi nodded silently. "We would be much happier without him," she said. "He is a mean and terrible giant."

Ahas took Tutubi home on his back, and then he began thinking of a plan. I will ask Tuko, Paparo, and Goyam to help me, he decided. Together we can punish that giant.

Early the next morning, Ahas told the others of his plan.

Tuko the Lizard said, "Of course I will help."

Paparo the Butterfly fluttered her wings excitedly. "Yes!" she said. "Let's go today."

Goyam the Ant also agreed to help. "I will do anything you say to get rid of that horrible Lupit," he said.

The four friends climbed into half a coconut shell and crossed the river to get to Lupit's house. They waited until the giant left for the afternoon, and then they sneaked into his cold, empty house.

"Tuko," Ahas said, "you go into his bathroom. And you, Goyam, wait in his rocking chair." Tuko and Goyam did as they were told.

"I know what to do," said Paparo, who knew the plan very well. "I'll wait in the kitchen."

Taking the rock in both hands, the hermit carefully lifted it out of the moist soil. Underneath he found two fat, wriggling worms. "Uh, hello," the hermit said to them. "Are you caught under this rock?"

"Not at all," one of the worms said. "The rock won't hurt us, but you might."

"I won't hurt you," the hermit said gently. "I'll just step over you and be on my way."

"Oh, that's right," said the worm angrily. "On your way to crush other poor creatures under your feet."

The hermit scratched his beard. "Huh?"

"You're human," the worm went on. "All humans treat the rest of us like we're worthless. You don't respect other living things, you cut down trees, and you pollute the environment."

"Hmmm," the hermit said, thinking, "Maybe you're right. Humans do destroy nature." Then, after a moment, he added, "Would you like to do something about it?"

"Like . . .?" the worm replied.

"I can turn you and your friend into humans," the hermit said, "so that you can live among people and teach them how to respect our planet."

After talking about it some more, the worms agreed to the experiment. Then—POOF!—they instantly turned into a man and a woman.

The new couple went on to live in a small farming village, where they were known as Gino and Ana Flores. With the money the hermit gave them, they bought some land and built a modest thatched-roof house. They also bought several sows and a few chickens.

At first Gino and Ana worked hard on their farm and made many new friends. Every chance they had, they talked to their friends about the richness and beauty of their former home, the rainforest, and they traveled to other towns to teach people about treating nature with respect and kindness.

The Battle of the Wind and the Rain

One clear day, Thunder, Lightning, and Rain were resting among the fluffy clouds that dotted the sunny sky. Wind played among them, gracefully dancing round and round, shifting the patterns in the sky ever so slightly.

"I'm bored," Wind announced. "Let's make a storm."

"We just made a huge one the other day," Lightning pointed out, "and I'm tired."

"Oh, you're always tired," said Wind. "You're just not as strong as I am."

"Fine," Lightning said. "I'm not."

"What about you, Thunder?" Wind said. "Do you want to stir up something exciting?"

"No," Thunder answered. "I'd rather wait until Lightning is ready."

Wind whirled around them a little faster, causing the clouds to move across the blue sky rather suddenly.

"Hey!" Rain said irritably. "Stop that. We're trying to sleep."

Wind laughed, and blew one big gust at Rain. "So make me stop," he said.

A little while later, Wind said, "Ha! You can't do it either. I guess nobody wins this contest."

"No, wait," Rain said. "I haven't tried the eastern rains." The stronger eastern rains then began to strike down on the poor monkey, who was already very wet. Big fat drops were hitting him on the head, and he had to shut his eyes to keep the water out. Finally, the monkey climbed down to the ground and scampered off to look for cover.

"I won!" Rain said triumphantly. "I beat you."

Wind, who looked almost as upset as the monkey, turned his back on Rain and flew off without saying a word. He, the most powerful of all elements, had actually lost to Rain. And now, just as he had promised, he would have to flee whenever he saw her.

That's why, when the winds are very strong, people always pray for rain. Once the rain comes, the wind always dies down and everything becomes more peaceful.

Alunsina

Long before there were animals and people, a gentle and loving god named Langit lived in the highest part of heaven with his wife, the goddess Alunsina. At the time the world was just a jumble of floating dust, rocks, soil, and water droplets, and it was Langit's wish to make order of all the pieces. He wanted to make a place that would be comfortable for the living creatures he planned to create later on.

"I'm going to form land masses with water surrounding them," Langit told Alunsina one morning. "The job will take a long time to finish, so I will be away for many days. Would you like to come along and help me?"

Alunsina drew a gold comb through her long wavy hair. "Do you really need me?" she said. "You know how I don't like long journeys."

Langit frowned. Although he loved Alunsina, he wished she had more energy to work alongside him. "Wait here, then," he said, kissing her on the cheek. "I have to go to work."

Alunsina watched as Langit flew across the sky, disappearing into the distance. Then she combed her hair until it shone and adorned herself with sweet perfume and sparkling jewelry. First she fastened a string of diamonds around her slender neck. She slipped colorful rings and gold ornaments onto each of her delicate fingers. She wrapped her wrists in strings of luminous pearls. Then, finally, she placed on her head her most prized possession—a golden crown.

Alunsina gazed at herself in the mirror, pleased. She was beautiful! If only Langit were around, she thought, everything would be perfect. She didn't understand why he had to leave her. Why did he have to work when they already had everything they could ever want? With a heavy sigh, Alunsina put away her jewelry and her gold comb. Then she drifted off to sleep.

The following day Alunsina took a long walk and played among the clouds. It wasn't much fun without Langit, though, so she went home and again combed her hair and tried on her jewelry. She did the same the next day and the next and the next.

After one week Alunsina began to grown restless and bored. She missed Langit's company, and she was beginning to doubt his love for her. Maybe he didn't really love her. Maybe he wasn't really working. Maybe he wanted to create a new wife!

Sick with worry, Alunsina summoned Wind. "I want you to find my husband and report to me what he's doing," she said. "And make sure he doesn't see you."

Wind looked at the goddess, puzzled.

"Please. He could be in great danger," she said, lying.

Wind didn't seem convinced, but he did as Alunsina wished and took off in search of Langit. He found Langit among the mountains and cliffs he had just built, towering rock formations that reached up to the heavens. Wind stayed several hours, and from his hiding place he watched as Langit gathered rocks of different shapes and sizes, creating more and more magnificent structures. Satisfied, Wind decided to go back to Alunsina.

Woosh! Wind took off, leaving behind him a plume of dust.

Langit looked up, feeling the breeze behind him. "Wind!" he called out. "I didn't know you were there. What are you doing?"

Wind stopped in his tracks, and the air became still. "I was just . . . aahhh," he said, stalling.

"Well . . ." Langit said.

"Alunsina was worried about you," Wind explained. "She sent me to check on you in case you were in danger."

"Danger?" Langit said, confused. "I'm not in any danger."

Wind remained silent. He didn't want to tell Langit that Alunsina had asked him to spy on him.

Langit gave Wind a stern look. "Did she ask you to hide from me, too?"

Wind nodded silently. "Yes," he said, ashamed.

Langit scowled. "Go back to Alunsina," he said, "and tell her that she must leave our home at once. She is lazy and selfish, and she doesn't understand my work."

Many days later Langit returned to his home. Alunsina was gone, and everything around him seemed dull and lifeless. He missed Alunsina's sweet perfume and her gentle kisses. He tried very hard to fight the loneliness in his heart, but when he couldn't bear it any longer, he went out to find her. He searched day and night for several months, but she was gone.

Finally, to forget his sorrow, he decided to plant trees and flowers on the lands he had made. He created fish to fill the sea, and animals to bring life to the earth. Then he took his wife's jewels and scattered them across the sky. Alunsina's diamond necklace made strings of stars, her gold comb shone in the form of a half-moon, her round luminous pearls made planets, and her crown became the sun.

Langit hoped that Alunsina would see all the beauty he created and return home, but she never did. To this day Langit sits alone in his palace in the sky. Sometimes he sheds tears of loneliness, which fall upon the earth as raindrops. Sometimes he calls out for her, his voice echoing across the sky much like thunder.

A Feast of Gold

There once lived a very rich couple who owned a large farm, or an *hacienda*, with endless fields of tall sugarcane. On the *hacienda* they had a big house with twenty-four servants. Though the house was grand, it was very bare. The couple didn't care about decorating their house or making it comfortable; all they cared about was money, money, and more money. From the moment they woke up in the morning to the time they went to bed, all they did was count their gold.

One day, when they were busy counting their money, a servant came to tell them that lunch was ready.

"Not now!" the man cried out, piles of gold all around him. "We're busy."

"The food can wait!" the woman said.

The servant turned and left. Two hours later, the couple finally came down to eat. But when they arrived at the table, they discovered that all the food had turned to gold. "Ohh!" the woman squealed in delight.

The man grabbed a fistful of gold coins and let them fall, one by one, onto his plate. "They're real," he said, smiling. "We're even richer than before." Then he took his wife into his arms and they danced all around the dining room.

"Let's celebrate with a feast," the woman said, clapping her hands.

"Yes," agreed her husband. "We'll call everyone we know."

"Lidya!" the woman yelled for the chief cook. "Lidya!"

The cook came to the door. "Yes, ma'am."

"Tonight we're having a celebration," the woman said. "Prepare a feast for three hundred guests."

The cook nodded. "Yes, ma'am." She went back into the kitchen, but a few seconds later she came back, a look of shock on her face. "Ma'am," she said, "I've just been to the pantry, and all our supplies have turned to gold!"

"What?" the couple said at once.

"All the food," said the cook in disbelief, "the sugar, the milk, the dried fish . . . everything's gone."

The man and the woman quickly ran into the pantry to see for themselves, and just as the cook said, it was overflowing with gold. "Yiheeeee!" said the woman, giving her husband a kiss. "More gold!"

The man wrapped his arms around her waist, grinning from ear to ear. "It will take months for us to count all this money." He laughed joyfully. "Maybe even years!"

"We'll postpone the celebration, then," the woman said. "We have too much work to do." She then grabbed a brown rice sack, which was now filled with gold, and began dragging it into the dining room. "Let's start counting."

Forgetting their hunger, the couple poured all their gold into one room and counted for several days. They didn't eat, they didn't sleep, and they didn't even speak to one another. Only the sound of tinkling coins could be heard echoing throughout their empty house, day after day and night after night. With each passing hour, they grew weaker and weaker from hunger, but they went on counting anyway.

Many times, the servants tried to bring in new supplies from the outside, but any food that was brought in instantly turned to gold. For their own meals, they were forced to eat at a neighbor's house.

Still, in spite of how thin the couple had become, and how faint they felt, they continued to carefully stack the gold coins, counting each and every last one. The thought that they should simply stop counting and go out to eat never even entered their minds because they had become blinded by gold.

The couple went on in this manner for weeks, neither one strong enough to break the spell of greed. Eventually, both died from starvation, without even enjoying their riches.

The Runaways

Tonito and his younger sister, Lupe, lived with their father in a little house on stilts. Their mother died when Lupe was just six months old, so the children didn't really remember her. But they had happy and healthy lives—that is, until their father decided to marry another woman who had a daughter named Gina.

Gina was very spoiled. She wore her hair in a long braid that reached down to her waist, with ribbons that always matched her dress. She was plump and a bit clumsy, and she cried whenever she didn't have her way, even though she was already five years old. Tonito and Lupe tried to play with her, but she didn't like to share her toys with them, and her mother yelled at them whenever Gina's clothes got dirty or if she tripped and fell in the garden. In fact, it seemed that whenever anything went wrong, it was either Tonito's or Lupe's fault.

One morning Gina picked all the *sampagita* flowers off her mother's favorite bush. When her mother came out of the house to fetch water from the pump, she discovered the fragrant flowers strewn about the garden, with Gina playing nearby.

"Gina!" she yelled, pointing at the scattered flowers. "Who did this to my *sampagitas*?"

Gina looked up at her mother but didn't answer.

"Did Lupe do this?" her mother asked.

"No," Gina said, afraid.

"Did Tonito do this?"

Gina looked down at her feet. "Yes," she said softly, even though it was not true.

Gina's mother frowned, then she turned back to the house to find Tonito. "Tonito!" she shouted, climbing up the ladder to their house.

Tonito and Lupe were lying on the floor on their bellies, drawing pictures. Tonito jumped up when he heard his name.

"You've completely destroyed my *sampagita* bush," Gina's mother said, pinching Tonito's ear. "No dinner for you tonight."

"No!" Tonito protested. "I didn't do it. Really I didn't."

"And you're a liar too," Gina's mother said, twisting his ear. Then she dragged him to the closet, pushed him inside, and slammed the door shut. "Don't come out until I say so," she said.

Lupe didn't dare say a word. She remained lying on the floor, pretending to draw. She knew that if she tried to help Tonito, she would be shoved in the closet too. But a few minutes after Gina's mother left, when Lupe was sure she was gone, she quietly cracked open the closet door. "Tonito," she whispered. "Tonito."

"Go away," Tonito answered, "or else you'll get in trouble."

"Please, Tonito," Lupe said. "Come out. I want to leave this place, and I want you to come with me."

42

"We can't leave," Tonito said. "Where would we go?"

Lupe opened the closet a little wider.

"We can run away, Tonito. Then she'll be sorry."

Tonito was silent for a while. "But what about Papa?" he said with a sniffle. "We can't leave him."

"But she's so mean," Lupe said. "I hate her! And, besides, Papa's always working. He won't even notice we're gone."

Tonito let out a heavy sigh. "Okay. Maybe he'll understand."

The very next day, before the sun came up, Tonito gently shook his sister awake. Then, without a word to each other, they quickly changed into their day clothes. They had to be very careful not to wake up Gina, their father, and their stepmother, who were all sound asleep on straw mats laid out on the floor.

43

Lupe and Tonito quietly slipped down a ladder from their house, the light from the moon guiding them. Then they began a long trek through the rice paddies, over a hill, and into the woods. They walked for so long that one of Tonito's slippers broke and he had to walk the rest of the way barefoot. By midafternoon they were thirsty and exhausted. They had already finished the rice and fish they brought along, and they had no water left.

Soon they came upon a big house on a riverbank. All the windows were shut, and the surrounding trees and plants were overgrown. "I don't think anyone lives here," Tonito said. "Let's go inside."

Lupe didn't think they should go in, but her stomach was grumbling, and she was tired of walking around with nowhere to go. She followed her brother around the side of the house, and they found a door leading into a spacious kitchen. On the stove they found a pot of vegetable stew. It was cold and didn't look very good, but Tonito and Lupe were so hungry, they didn't care how it tasted or that it might belong to someone else. Within minutes, they had eaten every bit of it.

Suddenly a tall, dark figure burst through the kitchen door. Lupe screamed and dropped the empty pot. It was a man dressed in animal skins, and he had a snout where his mouth should be. "Rarrrr!" he growled at the children.

"Run!" Tonito shouted, pushing his sister away from the man. Then he picked up the pot, hurled it at the man, and ran after Lupe, who was already climbing out a window.

Lupe jumped to the ground outside and looked up at her brother. "Hurry!" she cried. "Jump." The children ran from the house as fast as they could, but then they reached the river and could go no further.

"Ay!" Tonito said, looking behind him. "He's coming after us."

"Let's climb this tree," Lupe said, stepping on a large rock. "We can hide in the leaves."

They settled on a branch and huddled together. "Shhh," Tonito said, putting a finger to his lips. Lupe pulled her knees up to her chest, hardly breathing. Before long they heard twigs breaking and the crunch of dry leaves. The beastly man was coming closer and closer.

"Rarrrr!"

The man was suddenly beneath them, and in an instant he was clambering up the tree. "Oh, no!" Lupe said in panic. She looked down and saw that the man's outstretched hand could almost touch her.

Tonito pulled himself up to the branch above them. "Lupe!" he said, reaching down, "take my hand."

But instead Lupe pulled a mango off the tree. Thinking quickly, she threw it at the man. It missed, but when the mango splashed into the water below, he glanced down at the river, distracted.

"Ahhh!" he said, losing his grip and falling. He hit his head against a rock with a loud thud, then rolled into the river.

Silently the children watched as the current carried him off. Then they climbed down to the ground and went back to the man's house. "What do we do now?" Lupe asked Tonito. "Do you want to go home?"

"Do you?" Tonito asked.

Lupe stuck out her lower lip and shook her head. "No. She's so mean to us," she said, "and Gina is horrible too."

Tonito nodded sadly. "And Papa can't seem to do anything about it. He already knows we're not happy." He lay down on the floor next to his sister. "I guess we can stay here for a while." Then the children closed their eyes and drifted off to sleep.

The next morning Lupe and Tonito went outside and sat under the shade of the very same tree the man had fallen from. After a breakfast of sweet, juicy mangoes, they took a walk along the river. "Look," Tonito said, his eyes widening. There was a person drinking from the river several yards away.

Lupe squinted her eyes against the sun, and studied the figure for several moments. Her face broke into a smile and she squealed with excitement. "Papa!" she shouted. "Papa!"

The person stood up from a crouched position, and looked at the children. "Lupe!" he answered. "Tonito!"

The children ran toward their father and threw their arms around him. "What are you doing here?" Tonito asked.

"I've been so worried about you children," he said. "I had to find you. Why did you leave?"

Lupe took a step back. Pouting, she said, "Because we hate it at home. We're always punished for things we didn't do."

"Yes, yes, I thought so," her father replied softly. "And I'm so sorry I let that happen."

His eyes filled with tears, and he took Lupe's hand. "Let's go home. I won't let it happen again."

Lupe shook her head, and pulled her hand away from her father. "We want to stay here," she said stubbornly.

"Please come home with me," her father said gently. "Things will be better. I promise."

"But what about Gina and her mother?" Tonito said. "How can you make them be nice to us?"

Their father sighed. "I've thought this over carefully," he said, "and if Gina and her mother are making you so miserable, well, I . . ." his voice trailed off. "We can start over again, just the three of us."

"Really?" Lupe and Tonito said at once, their faces brightening.

Their father nodded and wrapped an arm around each of the children. "Yes. Now let's go home."

The Magic Lake

Pedro sang as he walked up the winding path leading into the forest, his old ax slung over his shoulder.

> "Deep into the woods I go
>   where wild flowers grow.
> With my ax I make firewood
> to sell in my neighborhood,
>   since seven years ago."

He was a poor woodcutter, and every morning he left his wife and children to chop firewood, which he sold at the market in the afternoons. He soon noticed a fallen tree by a lake.

"Perfect!" he said. "I won't even have to cut down this tree."

He got to work right away, swinging his ax with mighty blows. *Whack! Whack! Whack!* He was working as quickly as he could, wiping the sweat from his brow from time to time. The sun was beating down on his back, and he wanted to finish the job quickly so that he could get to the market early. But as he raised his ax to take another swing, its blade suddenly slipped off and flew into the lake behind him.

"Oh, no!" he said as the blade disappeared into the water with a big splash. Pedro had only one ax, and he didn't have enough money to buy a new one. Thinking quickly, he took off his shirt and dove into the water. He swam deeper and deeper, but he couldn't reach the bottom of the lake. He tried many more times, but he just couldn't find the blade.

As he sat under the shade of a tree, worrying about how he was going to pay for another ax, a beautiful fairy rose up from the water and magically appeared before him. Pedro gasped at the sight of her. Her hair reached down to her ankles, and her eyes expressed purity and kindness.

"What's wrong?" she asked.

Pedro stood up and hastily put his shirt back on. He explained what had just happened, then the fairy swiftly dove into the lake and emerged with an ax blade that shone brightly in the sun. It was made of pure silver.

"Is this it?" the fairy asked.

The woodcutter knew that if he took the blade, he would be the richest man in the local neighborhood or *barrio* as it was called. But Pedro shook his head and said, "No, that's not mine."

The fairy dove into lake again. Soon she reappeared holding a blade of shining gold. "Is this it?" she asked.

Again the woodcutter thought of how much money he would get for the solid gold blade, but he shook his head and said, "No, that's not it either."

Once again the fairy dove into the water and surfaced, this time holding Pedro's old iron blade. "Is this it?"

"Yes!" Pedro exclaimed. "That's mine." Delighted, he took the blade from the fairy. "Thank you so much."

"I admire your honesty," she said to Pedro. "Because you are an honest man, I would like to give you the silver blade and the gold one too."

The woodcutter's face brightened. "Really?" he said. "But those might belong to someone else."

"No," the fairy said. "I created these blades for you."

Pedro thanked the fairy again, then immediately set off for home. He was excited to show his wife his gold and silver blades. "We can sell them," he told his wife when he arrived at their cottage. "And we can save the money for the children's schooling."

Pedro's wife was very pleased, and she shared the news with all the neighbors. That same night the woodcutter's story was known all over the *barrio*. Even the children were talking about the fairy and the gold and silver axes. Everyone was happy except for Pedro's neighbor Lito. He felt he deserved the gold and silver axes even more than Pedro did.

Early the next morning, Lito loosened the blades on two of his axes and headed off to the same spot by the lake. He began cutting down a tree, and just as he had planned, the blade flew off his ax and fell into the lake.

"Oh no!" he exclaimed. Then he grabbed his second ax and took a swing at the tree. That blade slipped off, too, splashing into the lake. "Oh!" he said. "Both my axes are ruined!" Then he sat down and pretended to cry.

Before long the fairy appeared and asked him why he was crying. Lito explained that his axes were broken and that their blades were buried in the lake. As expected, the fairy dove into the water.

She appeared first with a silver blade. "Is this yours?" she asked Lito.

"You found it!" Lito said, pretending to be surprised. "What a good diver you are. Do you think you can find the other one?"

The fairy dove in again and came up with a gold blade. "Is this it?" she asked.

"Yes! Yes!" he said, holding out his hands greedily. "That's mine too."

But the fairy held on to both blades and said, "You shall have neither of these blades. I help only those who are honest. Get out of my woods quickly and never come back!" Then she vanished.

Lito had no choice but to go home feeling very much ashamed. "I'm not any richer, and I've even lost my two axes," he said to himself. "I wish I had been wiser and hadn't been so greedy."

The deer laughed again, making Bembol even more annoyed than he already was.

"Fine," said the deer. "My name is Gaspar, and I will race you when the sun comes up in the morning."

"I'm Bembol," said Bembol. "I'll be waiting for you by the old *banaba* tree on the other side of this stream."

That night Bembol gathered all his snail friends and told them what had happened. "How am I going to beat him?" he said worriedly. "What was I thinking when I challenged him?"

"Gaspar is very fast," said one of the older snails. "He's probably the fastest deer on the island."

Bembol's heart sank. His friends weren't making him feel any better. He wanted to beat Gaspar more than anything in the world, but it was true, he didn't even have legs or feet. How was he going to do it?

But as they talked some more, the snails began to think of ways to beat the deer. And by the end of the meeting, they had a very good plan.

The next morning three of Bembol's best friends positioned themselves along the racecourse, which began at the old *banaba* tree and ended at the top of a hill. The first snail went to the small guava orchard and waited there. The second snail waited at the wooden footbridge that crossed the stream. And the third snail posted himself on the fringes of the pineapple field. Bembol's friends all knew exactly what to do.

Bembol and Gaspar met at the old *banaba* tree by the stream. "Are you ready to lose?" Gaspar said to Bembol with a smirk.

Bembol didn't answer. Instead he positioned himself at the starting line and waited for the signal to begin the race.

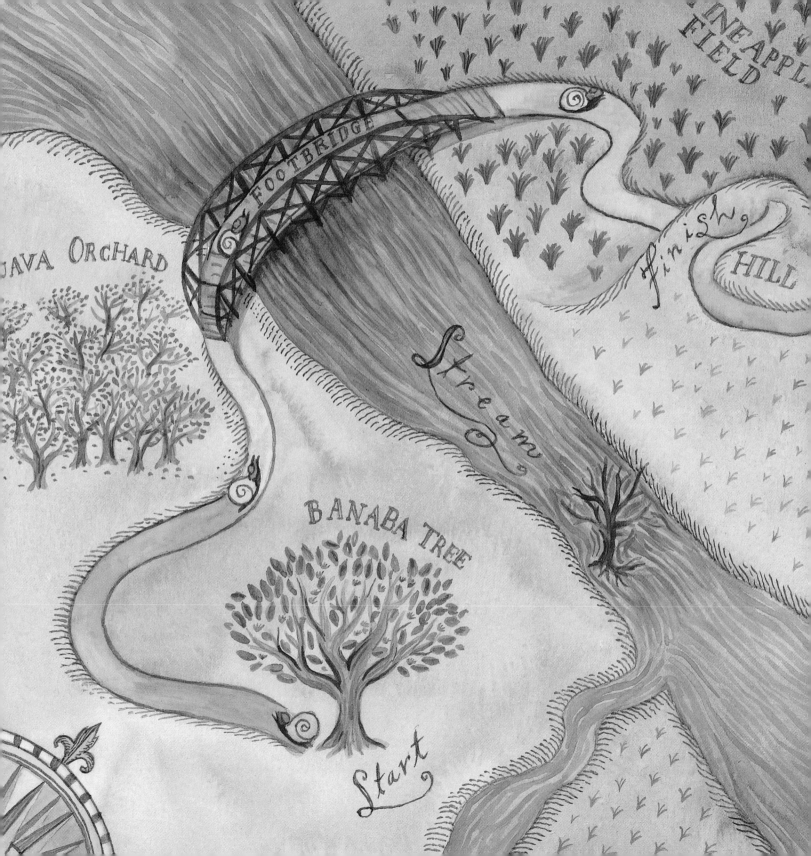

"On your marks," one of Gaspar's deer friends began, "get set . . . GO!"

Bembol took off as fast as he could, but Gaspar only stood back and watched him. "Ha, ha, ha!" he said, laughing. "Is that the best you can do? Even my grandmother can move faster than that!"

Bembol didn't look back, no matter what Gaspar said. If his plan worked, the haughty deer would be apologizing to him within the hour.

Soon Gaspar was far behind, but Bembol guessed that Gaspar had not even left the starting line yet. He was probably still chatting with his friends, drinking water from the stream, or smelling flowers along the way.

Bembol knew that Gaspar would be taking his time, bragging to all his friends that a snail was no match for him.

Then, when Bembol was about thirty meters away from the guava orchard, Gaspar finally passed him at an easy walk.

"Hah!" the deer said, glancing down at him. "Even with a head start, you're still going to lose!"

But Bembol wasn't worried. He knew that his snail friend, Tara, was waiting in the orchard. She would continue the race in his place while Bembol took a shortcut to the finish line. He positioned himself on the side of the track and watched with pleasure as Gaspar drew closer and closer to Tara.

"You'd better speed up, slowpoke," Tara said, pretending to be Bembol. "I'm going to win!"

Even from thirty meters away, Bembol could see that Gaspar seemed startled when he saw Tara in front of him. The deer stopped in his tracks for a moment or two, then he shook his head and picked up his pace, dashing ahead of Tara whom he thought was Bembol. This, of course, was exactly what was supposed to happen. The snails had planned everything very carefully.

Bembol slowly began to make his way to the finish line. He knew that his plan was going to work. When Gaspar arrived at the wooden footbridge, another one of his snail friends would be waiting—and Gaspar would think that Bembol was still ahead of him.

And when Gaspar got to the pineapple field, there would be another Bembol lookalike that would fool Gaspar once again.

Bembol couldn't help but smile as he slid along a tree that had fallen across the narrowest part of the stream. He was going to beat Gaspar and make him apologize once and for all!

On the other side of the stream, Bembol made a steep climb to the top of the hill, where the finish line was. There, just two feet away from the finish line, he waited for Gaspar to appear.

After a minute or two, Bembol heard pounding hooves coming his way. From the vibrations in the ground Bembol could tell that Gaspar was galloping toward the finish line.

As quickly as he could Bembol began inching his body forward, pushing and pulling his muscles rhythmically.

Although Gaspar was far away, Bembol knew that the deer could still overtake him. He looked back and saw Gaspar crossing the bridge that led up to the final stretch. He saw that the deer had spotted him and was running as fast as he could to catch up.

Bembol pushed and pulled and pushed and pulled, faster and faster—until, finally, he crossed the finish line!

A second later Gaspar galloped past him. His coat was covered with foamy sweat, and his underside was heaving.

"I won!" Bembol exclaimed. "I beat you!"

Gaspar didn't say a word. Out of breath and panting, he was totally exhausted from his final sprint. His head was pounding, his body felt weak, and he was seeing stars dancing in front of his eyes.

His forelegs began to fold, followed by his hind legs, and the next thing he knew, he was lying in a heap on the grass.

"I won!" Bembol said again.

His only reply was Gaspar's panting.

"You have to apologize to me now," Bembol insisted.

Gaspar opened his mouth as if to speak, but instead of speaking, he took a long, deep breath.

"Well?" Bembol said, waiting. "Say you're sorry for throwing a stone at me."

"Apologize."

"Sorry," Gaspar finally said weakly. Then he closed his eyes and passed out.

A Bridge of Flowers

A long time ago, Bathala (as God was known to Filipinos in ancient times) asked his messenger to gather all his children for a special meeting. His daughters arrived in heaven first: Tala, the morning star; Liwayway, the dawn; and Tag-ani, the goddess of the harvest. Then, not five minutes later, Bathala's sons arrived: Hangin, the wind; Kidlat, lightning; and Araw, the sun.

His three sons and three daughters promptly took their seats at the big oval table in the main hall of heaven's palace, waiting for the meeting to begin. They knew that something important was about to take place.

Bathala smiled as he watched his children take their seats, proud of each and every one of them. But then he noticed that his youngest daughter's seat was still empty. "Where's Bighari?" he asked, scowling. "She's not coming . . . again?"

The messenger hesitated for a moment, avoiding her steady gaze. "Well, uh," he began, "he sent me here to tell you that . . . that . . . you must never come home again."

"But, but why?" Bighari said, confused. "What have I done? Is he angry with me?"

"Yes, mistress," was all the messenger could say.

"But why?"

The messenger took a deep breath. "Because you were absent at today's meeting."

"What meeting?" Bighari said, genuinely surprised.

"He called for a special meeting," the messenger explained. "I looked everywhere for you . . ." His voice trailed off.

"I'm so sorry," he continued. "You have been banished from heaven."

"But I didn't know." She looked at the messenger, her round brown eyes filled with tears. "I didn't know!"

"I'm very sorry," the messenger said again. "There are too many gardens. I just couldn't find you in time."

"I've made my father unhappy once again," Bighari said, crying. "And I promised . . . Oh, so many times I promised to stay closer to home!" She was sobbing now, and the messenger turned to leave her.

"I wish you well, my mistress," the messenger said before he disappeared into the blackness surrounding them.

Bighari cried bitterly for many hours, until the sun came up. She thought about going to her father to change his mind, but she knew it would do no good. Instead, she set about making the garden her new home, hoping that in time her father would forgive her. She made friends with the people and the animals who lived nearby, and she created thousands of varieties of flowers. Never before had anyone seen the colors she brought into the world with every new blossom. Never before had anyone smelled the scents produced by the flowers.

Then, one day, Bighari decided to build a giant bower made of flowers, one that arched across the sky and could be seen even by those who lived far away. The blossom-covered monument reached way up into the sky. Green, blue, red, orange, yellow—these were a few of the colors of Bighari's bower.

Secretly she hoped her father would see the magnificent arch and invite her back to heaven. Many years later, he did just that.

Today, when we are especially lucky, we can still see Bighari's bower. But we have given it a different name. We call it a rainbow.

Why the Cock Crows

The Philippines of ancient times was made up of many different tribes. Fights and disagreements always arose between the tribes, so the god of war, named Sidapa, had a very difficult job. He had to settle all the fights brought to his attention by messengers of the people. Outside Sidapa's office there was always a line of messengers waiting to talk to him because tribal wars broke out every day.

One night Sidapa was working especially late because a woman had been kidnapped from her village by a neighboring tribe. Though he was very tired, Sidapa couldn't rest until he had devised a plan that would return her home safely.

"Pepe," he said to one of his soldiers. "You must wake me up before sunrise. I have an important meeting in the morning and I'm afraid I won't be up in time."

"Yes, sir!" Pepe said.

"You go now," Sidapa ordered. "I want you to go to bed at once so that I can be sure you will not oversleep."

As instructed, Pepe turned to leave for his quarters. But as he walked by the line of people outside Sidapa's office, he saw some of his friends and decided to stop and talk to them for a few minutes. Maybe they would be interested in hearing the latest news about the woman who had been kidnapped, he thought. Pepe knew all the details of the kidnapping because he had spent most of the evening in Sidapa's office.

Before long, Pepe was deeply engaged in gossip with the waiting messengers. "My boss says he will send in his army if they don't release her by one o'clock in the morning," he told the men gathered around him. "And he is planning a sneak attack from . . ." He paused. "I can't tell you that."

Pepe covered his mouth with his hand, as if to shut himself up, and the circle of men tightened around him.

"Tell us," one messenger said.

"Come on, Pepe," added another. "We promise not to tell anyone."

"Yes," someone else chimed in. "Please tell us!"

Pepe looked at all the eager faces around him, and felt very important. Everyone seemed so interested in what he had to say. They were really listening to him!

"Well, okay," he said slowly, "but this is a secret. You must not tell anyone."

All the men nodded. "We won't tell," they promised. "We won't tell."

Pepe took a deep breath and described in great detail Sidapa's secret plan for getting the woman back from her captors. Then the clock struck midnight, and Pepe rushed off to go to sleep. He had been having so much fun talking that he had forgotten the time. He rolled into bed and drifted off into a deep sleep. The next thing he knew, Sidapa was towering over him, yelling loudly.

"You lazy soldier!" the god of war shouted. "Wake up!"

Pepe blinked his eyes open upon hearing his boss's angry voice. To his surprise, the room was already bright with sunlight, and the sleeping mats around him had been rolled up and put away. "Sir!" he said, jumping to his feet.

"Do you know what time it is, soldier?" Sidapa said, shaking with anger.

"N-n-n-no, sir," he replied, stammering. Pepe could feel his knees trembling. He was very frightened.

"I am late for my meeting," Sidapa boomed. "You didn't do what I asked you to do. You're a worthless soldier!"

With that, Sidapa spun around and strode out the door.

For an instant Pepe couldn't move. He stood frozen in the same spot, his heart pounding inside him. Then suddenly he ran forward, chasing his commander.

"Great Sidapa, god of war," he said, falling to his knees, "please forgive me." Sidapa looked down at him through squinted eyes. "No! I'm going to punish you for this serious error."

"I tried to go to bed early," Pepe explained, "but the messengers stopped me and asked a thousand questions." Pepe felt terribly sorry, and he searched his mind to come up with a better excuse. But, having none, he decided to tell the truth. He confessed to Sidapa that he had been gossiping with his friends, and he even said that he had told them about the secret attack plan.

"Now you're in even more trouble than you were before!" Sidapa said, enraged. "You have no business telling people what you hear in my office."

Pepe's eyes filled with tears. "I am very sorry, sir," he said meekly.

"Your laziness and your big mouth will cost me a lot of trouble," the god said, fuming. "I am going to put a curse on you that will teach you and everyone else an important lesson."

"Oh, no!" Pepe begged. "Please, no."

"From now on," Sidapa continued, "you will not be able to speak, your body will shrink, you will grow wings and feathers, and every morning, before dawn, you will wake up and crow."

Pepe shook his head in disbelief. "But . . ."

Before he could finish his sentence, Pepe's mouth turned into a bird's beak, his body began to shrivel, his arms became wings, and—one by one—feathers sprouted all over his body. Ashamed by his appearance and fearful that Sidapa would make him even more deformed, he flew out of the palace.

Since then Pepe has been called a cock, and every morning he crows before dawn.

The Battle of the Sea and Sky

When time began, there was only the sky, the sea, and a single black bird. Because there was no land yet, the bird had no choice but to fly continuously through the air. She would streak across the sky, day after day, without rest. When her wings were tired, she would simply stretch them open as wide as she could, letting the wind lift and carry her for long distances.

One afternoon the bird grew so tired that she could barely open her wings to glide with the wind. But there was no place to rest. Beneath her was only the rolling blue waters of the vast sea. In her heart she knew that it would be only a matter of days before she would fall into the sea and drown. She had to think of a way to rest her weary wings; otherwise she would surely die.

In those days, the sky hung very low, nearly touching the sea.

"How can I use the sea and the sky to build something I can rest on?" she wondered.

After thinking about it for several days, she knew exactly what to do. She set about her plan as soon as the next day broke, and swooped down to the sea.

"The sky tells me," she said to the sea, "that you're a worthless body of salty water. You don't do anything but make useless waves. You can't even help me fly like the sky does."

"What?" the sea said, insulted. "The life in me runs deeper than the sky can ever imagine, and there is a world under my waves that is much richer than anything in the sky!"

"Well," said the bird, "the sky says you are a good-for-nothing, and that you will one day drown me."

The bird's report angered the sea. In an instant the waters turned black and began to churn, and large waves began to rise up toward the sky. Bigger and bigger the waves grew, frothy white foam forming at their crests. The deep roar of the rushing waters was as loud as thunder.

Quickly the bird flew out of the way, afraid that one of the waves would snatch her out of the sky and drown her. She watched from a safe distance as the sea sent its waves higher and higher. It seemed that the sea was using all its strength to drown the sky!

The sky swiftly pulled itself out of reach, rising up to the heavens. But the sea reached farther up to the sky, finally crashing into the sky with its salty wetness. Then, suddenly, a bolt of lightning struck down at the sea, and rocks and boulders began to rain down from the darkening sky.

The bird nervously flit from right to left, up and down, trying her best to stay out of danger's way. There were rocks flying in every direction, and her feathers were beginning to feel heavy with seawater.

"Oh, no! What have I done?" she said to herself. "I'm in even more danger than I was before!"

Then, as suddenly as it all began, everything stopped. Cautiously the bird sailed through the sky, which was once again quiet, bright, and blue. Looking down at the sea, she saw formations in it that weren't there before.

She flew down closer to get a better look, noticing that the sea was now much farther away from the sky. Giant rocks grouped together in clusters filled the sea, and they jutted out above the water's surface. The waves had quieted down, though they were crashing against the rocks at the edges of every cluster.

Curiously she watched as the water around the formations moved toward the rocks, then away, and then back again. Then, when she was sure the sea wouldn't suddenly rise up in anger, she drifted down lower and lightly touched her feet to a rock at the highest point. The surface felt solid and secure. At last, she thought, a place to rest!

From her perch she looked all around her. As far as she could see, there were rock formations rising up from the sea. Some were large, some only tiny outcrops jutting out of the water. As they grew and settled, they became the islands that form the Philippine archipelago, which even today includes more than seven thousand islands.

The Prince's Bride

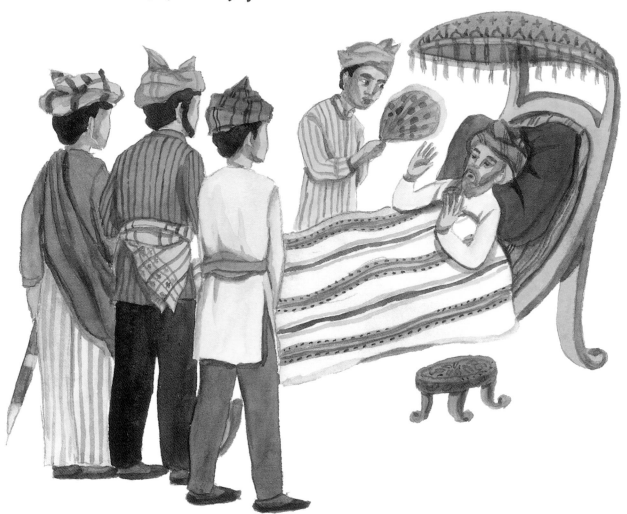

"I want to see all of you married before I die," the old king said to his three sons, who were gathered by his bedside. The king's forehead was slick with perspiration, and his voice was barely above a whisper. He had been sick for many months, and every day he grew weaker.

"Now, go," he said hoarsely, "go and search for your wives."

Marco gently laid Berta down on a rocking chair. Then, calmly, he approached his father's bed. "Father," he said in a serious tone, "I respect you and I don't want to make you unhappy."

He paused, glancing back at the caterpillar. "But Berta is a magical creature. I know she looks like caterpillar, but she speaks as intelligently as any woman I have ever met."

The king grunted, and turned his head away from his son.

"More importantly," Marco said, "she loves me, and I love her." Marco reached over and put a hand on his father's shoulder. "Father, please listen."

The king, who was a fair and loving father, slowly turned over to face his son.

"I would be the happiest man alive . . . No, I am the happiest man alive because of her," Marco said. "Please, I beg you, give us your blessing."

The king remained silent for long time. When he finally spoke, he seemed tired and sad. "You are a fool," he told Marco, "but if you don't mind that the whole town will laugh at you, then you can do as you wish."

"Oh! Thank you, Father," Marco said, kissing the king's hand. "I'm very grateful!"

The next day the king announced that the wedding would take place in three days in order to give the brides enough time to weave their own veils. As part of the traditional Filipino wedding ceremony, the veils would be draped around each couple as a symbol of their unity. The brides immediately got to work on their veils, as three days was little time to weave a cloth broad enough to be wrapped around two people.

Manuel's bride wove a delicate cloth using silk and pineapple fibers, called *sutlang pinya*. Paolo's bride produced a sturdy fabric made from wild-banana leaves, called *abaka*, which she then dyed crimson.

On the wedding day the veils were displayed on the backs of each couple's carriage for all the townspeople to see. As the wedding procession slowly floated down the town's main street, cries of approval rose up from the crowd:

"God bless you!"

"She's beautiful!"

"Best of luck to you both!"

"May you have many children."

But neither of the exquisite veils could compare to the lush silk Berta wove. Yards and yards of the colorful silk adorned Marco's carriage, every one of its brilliant threads gleaming brightly in the morning sun. Yet, even though the cloth was stunning, the crowd jeered when they saw Marco's caterpillar-bride.

"She's got more hair than you!" someone cried out to Marco.

"You should have married my goat!" another shouted, laughing.

"The youngest prince is blind!"

Marco lovingly stroked Berta's fuzzy neck. "It's all right, my sweet," he said in a soothing voice. "They can laugh all they want, and I'll still love you."

At the end of the procession the couples descended from their carriages and approached an outdoor altar that was set up for the ceremony. From a balcony above the altar the king watched. Manuel and Paolo stood proudly next to their brides throughout the mass.

Marco cradled Berta close to his chest, as though shielding her from harm. Finally the priest asked the couples to kneel down so that their veils could be wrapped around their shoulders.

As Marco began to kneel, Berta suddenly spoke. "Put me on the ground and crush me with your foot," she said.

Marco looked at her, alarmed. "What? Why?"

"Please, Marco," Berta whispered, "don't ask questions. Just trust me and do as I say."

"But—"

"Now, my Prince," the caterpillar-bride said urgently. "You have to do it before it's too late!"

Marco shook his head in bewilderment, but he gently set her on the ground as she asked. Then, closing his eyes tightly, he lifted his foot above her and brought it down just below her neck.

Even with his eyes closed, Marco saw a bright light suddenly flash before him, and he felt a gust of cool wind. He opened his eyes . . . in front him stood the most beautiful woman he had ever seen. He looked at her, astonished.

The crowd gasped in surprise. Marco's brothers could only stare. With her full red lips and almond-shaped eyes, the woman's magnificent beauty made the two other brides look like poor peasants.

"I'm free at last," the woman said to Marco, kissing him on the cheek. "Thank you."

Marco struggled to find his voice. "Who . . . who are you?"

The woman tossed back her long wavy hair, and laughed. "I'm Berta, of course," she said. "I was a princess once, but a witch cast a spell on me, and only the truest love from a prince could break it."

"Berta?" the young prince said in disbelief.

"Yes, my prince, it's really me."

Slowly a warm smile spread across Marco's face. "Berta! Why, you're perfect!" he cried.

The crowd burst into cheer as Marco took her in his arms and kissed her. The king stood up from his chair, clapping in delight.

By noon the three couples were married, and the whole town celebrated with a fiesta of dancing, singing, and succulent food. Eventually the king grew to love the caterpillar-princess more than his other daughters-in-law, and before he died, he left the throne to Marco, the youngest prince.

Select Bibliography

Aquino, Gaudencio V. *Philippine Myths and Legends*. Quezon City:
    National Book Store, 1992.

Aquino, Gaudencio V., Bonifacio N. Cristobal, and Delfin Fresnesa.
    Philippine Folktales. Quezon City: Alemar-Phoenix Publishing
    House, 1969.

Eugenio, Damiana L. *Philippine Folk Literature: The Myths*. Quezon City:
    University of the Philippines Press, 1993.

Fansler, Dean S. *Filipino Popular Tales*. Pennsylvania: Folklore Associates,
    Inc., 1965.

Jocano, F. Landa. *Myths and Legends of the Early Filipinos*. Quezon City:
    Alemar-Phoenix Publishing House, Inc., 1971.

Mallari, I.V. *Tales from the Mountain Province*. Manila: McCullough
    Printing Company, 1958.

Manuel, E. Arsenio. *A Treasury of Stories: Myths and Folktales*. Edited by
    Gilda Cordero-Fernando. Pasig City: Anvil Publishing Inc. and
    the National Commission on Culture and Arts, 1995.

Pasig Papers. Gilda Cordero-Fernando Collection. The Eugenio Lopez
    Library.

Ramos, Maximo. *Philippine Myths and Tales*. Manila: Bookman, Inc.,
    1957.

Sta. Romana-Cruz, Neni. *The Warrior Dance and Other Classic Philippine
    Sky Tales*, 1998.

Ventura, Sylvia Mendez. *The Carabao-Turtle Race and Other Classic
    Philippine Animal Folk Tales*. Manila: Tahanan Books for Young
    Readers, 1993.

Young, Johnny C. *101 Popular Local Myths and Legends*. Metro Manila:
    Johnny C. Young, 1996.